DOUG
THE BUG THAT WENT BOING!

For all the wonderful staff and children
at Blueberry Nursery

SIMON AND SCHUSTER
First published in Great Britain in 2013
by Simon and Schuster UK Ltd
1st Floor, 222 Gray's Inn Road, London, WC1X 8HB
A CBS Company

Text and illustrations copyright © 2013 Sue Hendra
By Paul Linnet and Sue Hendra

A CIP catalogue record for this book is available
from the British Library upon request

978-1-4711-1908-8 (HB)
978-0-85707-446-1 (PB)
978-1-4711-1844-9 (eBook)

Printed in China
1 3 5 7 9 10 8 6 4 2

DOUG
THE BUG THAT WENT BOING!

by Sue Hendra

SIMON AND SCHUSTER
London New York Sydney Toronto New Delhi

Doug and Trevor had been best friends for a long time. They played together every day and didn't like to be apart.

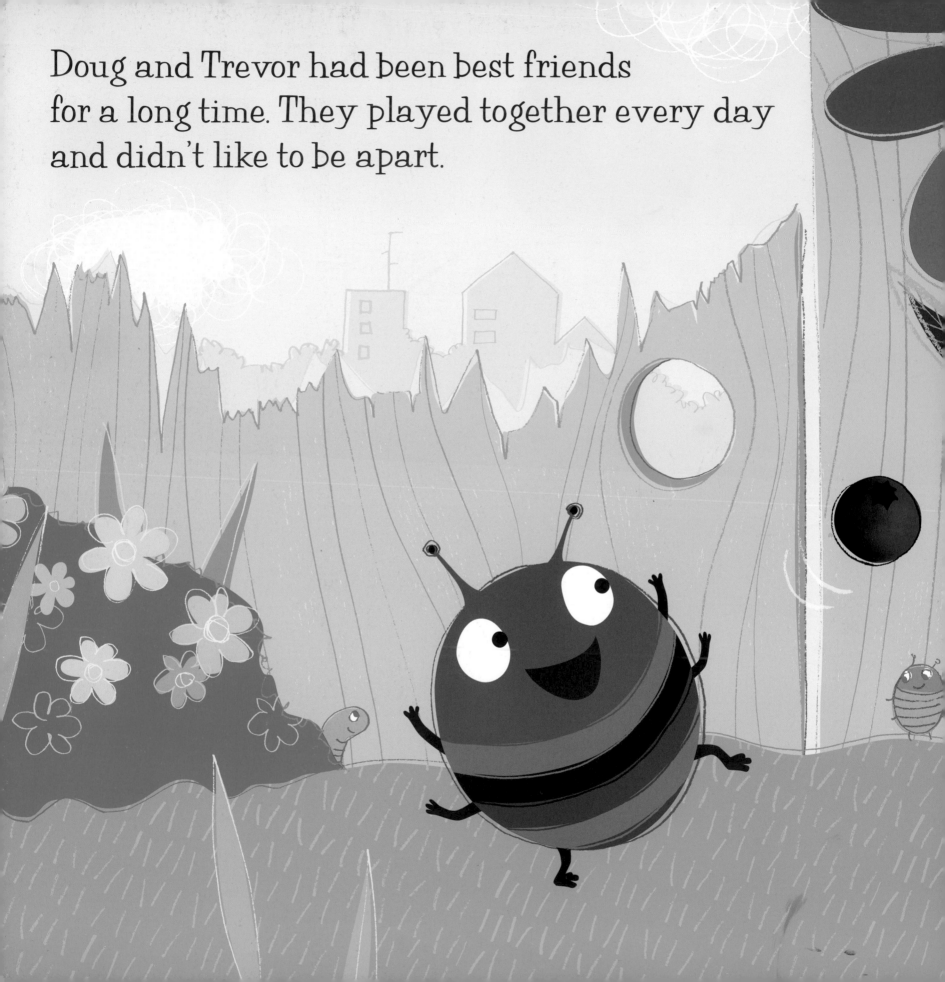

One day they were playing Berry Ball when . . .

Oh dear.

"Bad luck, Trevor," said Doug.
"It's your turn to get it down."

"Is not," said Trevor.

"Is too," said Doug.

"Is NOT!" said Trevor.

"You always make me climb up there," said Doug, crossly. "You always say it's my turn when it's not. I don't want to play any more."

"Fine," said Trevor. And he turned away in a huff.

But just then . . . .

. . . a great big shovel came down and scooped Doug up.

Oh no!
What on earth was happening?

"Doug!"
cried Trevor.

"Trevor!" cried Doug.

When he finally opened his eyes,
Doug got quite a surprise.

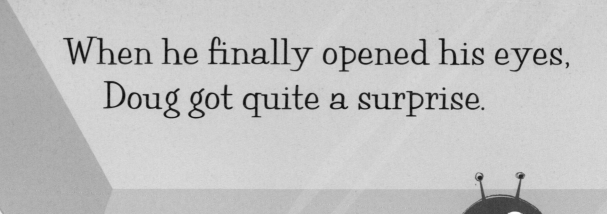

"TREVOR!" he yelled. "HELP!"

But Trevor was too far away to hear him.

"I've got to get home,"
thought Doug. But how?

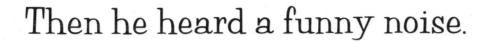

Then he heard a funny noise.

Bzzzz, bzzzz, bump!

It was a very dizzy fly. He was banging his head against the window.

Bzzzz, bzzzz, bump!

"Erm, maybe you should try the door," said Doug, politely.

"The door? Great idea! Why didn't I think of that? I've been here for days. Oh, how can I ever thank you?" said the fly.

Doug tried not to laugh. "Well," he said, "maybe you could take me with you?"

"I'll try," said the fly.
"You look quite heavy.
But here goes!"

Bzzzz, bzzzz . . .

...whoa!

"Don't drop me in there!" cried Doug.

Bzzzz, bzzzz ...

...whey!

"Or on there!" he gasped.

"And definitely **don't** drop me THERE!"

Phew! That was close.

But the fly was starting to wobble. "Don't . . . think . . . I . . . can . . . hold . . . on . . ."

And then -

PLOP!
Doug landed, SPLAT,
in somebody's breakfast.

He was just wondering if things could get any worse - when they did.

Pepper sprinkled onto his nose and—

aah,

aaah,

aaaah . . .

...choo!

Doug shot through the air
and span round and round
on the ceiling fan.

Then boing!

He bounced off a sponge cake

.... towards the toaster.

Ping!

He smashed through the toast
and began to fall.

He grabbed the first thing he could
and swung—

aargh!—

all the way back

. . . to exactly where he had started.

Doug had to admit things weren't going very well.

"Will I ever see Trevor again?" he said, sadly.

Then he heard a familiar sound . . .

"Bzzzz, bzzzz, byeeeee!" it called.
It was the fly, buzzing out of sight.
And that was when Doug noticed
that the window . . . WAS OPEN!

"Hey! Wait for me!" he called.
How was he going to get out now?

Then Doug had an idea . . .

Wheeeeee!

"Home I go!"
cried Doug.

The friends were so happy to see each other again.
"I'm sorry I wouldn't get the ball," said Trevor.
"I'm sorry I got so cross," said Doug.
     "Tell you what," said Trevor. "How about
a game of Berry Ball right now?"
     "You're on!" said Doug.

And all was well until . . .

oh no!
It happened again!

Doug looked at Trevor.
Trevor looked at Doug.

"I'll get it," said Trevor.

"Let me," said Doug.

"No, no, it's definitely
my turn," said Trevor.

And they were so busy arguing,
they didn't hear a familiar sound.

Bzzzz, bzzzz . . .

"CATCH!"
said the fly.

And they all played happily till the sun went down.

For Olga and Mambo

A TEMPLAR BOOK

This edition published in the UK in 2019 by Templar Books.
First published in the UK in 2018 by Templar Books,
an imprint of Bonnier Books UK,
The Plaza, 535 King's Road, London, SW10 0SZ
www.templarco.co.uk
www.bonnierbooks.co.uk

Text and Illustration copyright © 2018 by Ximo Abadía
Design copyright © 2018 by Templar Books

1 3 5 7 9 10 8 6 4 2

ISBN 978-1-78741-153-1 (hardback)
ISBN 978-1-78741-394-8 (paperback)
ISBN 978-1-78741-630-7 (ebook)

This book was typeset in ITC Avant Garde Gothic.
The illustrations were created with graphite,
wax and ink, and coloured digitally.

Edited by Joanna McInerney
Designed by Olivia Cook and Kieran Hood

Printed in China